the SCHOOLKIDS' JOKE BOOK

Compiled and edited by Brough Girling

Illustrated by Tony Blundell

Collins

An *Imprint of* HarperCollins*Publishers*

First published in Great Britain by Collins 1988
11 13 15 17 16 14 12

Collins is an imprint of HarperCollins*Publishers* Ltd,
77-85 Fulham Palace Road, Hammersmith,
London W6 8JB.

Text copyright © 1988 by Brough Girling
Illustrations copyright © 1988 by Tony Blundell

ISBN 0 00 692861-7

The author and illustrator assert the moral right
to be identified as the author and illustrator of this work.

Printed and bound in Great Britain by Caledonian
International Book Manufacturing Ltd, Glasgow, G64

What's black and white and read all over?

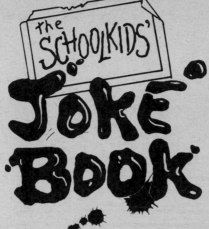

So says David Parfitt of Earby County School, Earby, Lancashire.

All the jokes and riddles in this book were collected, playground fresh, from schools in Britain (and forces schools in Germany) by Books for Students, the school paperback bookshop specialists.

They are all red hot favourites – some are old chestnuts, some are crispy new. There's something here for everyone, so hurry while stocks last!

The **STAR JOKES** have received special rewards – prizes of books have been sent to the jokers concerned, and their schools.

Well done to everyone who had their favourite jokes selected. Now we can all share them!

Brough Girling

What do you get?
What do you call?
and what goes . . .?

QUESTION: What do you get if you ask schoolkids to send you a lot of jokes?
ANSWER: A lot of jokes.

Here are just a few of the great what-do-you-get jokes you get . . .

What do you get if you dial 666?
The Australian police.

and

What do you get if you dial 000?
Nothing
Benjamin Randall, St Joseph's School, Poole

What do you get if you dial
34759624975938472649583774193?
A sore finger.
Susie Goodwin, Parkroyal School, Macclesfield

Now a world famous one:

What do you get if you cross a kangaroo with a sheep?
ALL TOGETHER: A woolly jumper.
Kelly Cox, Bruggen RAF School, Germany

What do you get if you cross a leopard with a sheep and a kangaroo?

A spotted woolly jumper.

Matthew Boulton, St Joseph's School, Poole

What do you get if you cross a penguin with a sheep and a kangaroo?

A black and white woolly jumper.

Joanne Barrow, Albany School, Nottingham

What do you get if you cross a kangaroo with a mink?

A fur jumper with pockets.

and

What do you get if you cross a pig with a zebra?
Striped sausages.
Samantha Craig, Fir Tree School, Leeds

What do you get if you cross a cow, a sheep and a goat?
A Milky Baa Kid.
Alison Boone, Booker Hill School, High Wycombe

What do you get if you cross a football team with an ice cream?
Aston Vanilla.
Paul Forsyth, Mountfield School, Newcastle

That's right, Paul – and they always get licked!

What do you get if you cross a bear with a skunk?
Winnie the Pooh.
Steven Burdett, Ryton School, Tyne and Wear

What do you get if you cross a ghost with a packet of crisps?
Crisps that go bump in the night.
Kerri Williams, Scargill School, Rainham

What do you get if you cross a skunk with a boomerang?
A nasty smell that you can't get rid of.
Kelvin Janson, Albany School, Nottingham

What do you get if you cross a cat with a chemist's?
Puss in Boots.
Natasha Mendis, St Mary's School, Hendon

What do you get if you roll a tomato down a hill?
Squashed tomato.
Laurie Phillips, Oerlinghausen School, Germany

What do you get if you jump out of Concorde without a parachute?
Shorter
Jonathan Porthouse, East Boldon School, East Boldon

What do you get if you cross a cow with a camel?
Lumpy milkshakes.
Malcolm Hiskey, Holland Park School, Clacton-on-Sea

What do you get if you cross a giraffe with a hedgehog?
An eleven metre hair brush.
Nyree Thornton, St Joseph's School, Poole

What do you get when you put your auntie in the fridge?
Aunti-Freeze
Michael Scott, Ryton School, Tyne and Wear

What do you get if you sit under a cow?
A pat on the head.
Alison Gray, Howes Down School, West Wickham

And my own favourite: What do you get if you cross a
  motorway with a pair of roller skates?
Run over.

AND NOW FOR SOME "WHAT DO YOU CALL" JOKES. . .

"What do you call a man . . ." jokes are fairly new.
  We didn't have them when I was at school – but that
  was so long ago we used to do dinosaur projects in
  Current Affairs! There are lots of these jokes – and
  they're spreading fast: soon the whole world will be
  knee-deep in them! Here are some of my favourites:

What do you call a man with rabbits down his trousers?
Warren

What do you call a man who swims round in circles in rivers?
Eddy

What do you call a girl with a foot on either side of a stream?
Bridget

What do you call a girl who gambles?
Betty

What do you call a man with a spade in his head?
Doug

What do you call a man without a spade in his head?
Douglas

Now here are some of yours:

What do you call a man who claps at Christmas?
Santapplause
Ravinder Purawal, Boleyn Road, Forest Gate

What do you call a bee with a quiet buzz?
A mumble bee.
Nadia Rahaman, Belleville School, London

What do you call a man who's always around when you want him?
Andy
Lynne Reynolds, Westwood School, Welling

What do you call a nun with a washing machine on her
  head?
Sistermatic
Amy Midgley, St Peter's School, Darwen

What do you call a man who can sing and drink lemonade
  at the same time?
A pop singer.
Charlie Garrad, Brooklands School, Bratham

What do you call a lady who doesn't like butter?
Marge
Amanda Richardson, Albany School, Nottingham

What do you call a man with an elephant on his head?
Squashed
Julie Fryer, Ryton School, Tyne and Wear

★ STAR JOKE ★ STAR JOKE ★ STAR JOKE ★

What do you call a deer with no eyes?
No eye deer.

What do you call a deer with no legs and no eyes?
Still no eye deer.
WELL DONE Paul Wills, St Mary's School, Hendon

What do you call a camel with three humps?
Humphrey.
Katie Neale, Clackclose School, Downham Market

What do you call a lady with two toilets?
Lou Lou.
Nadia Rahaman, Belleville School, London

What do you call a man who comes through your letter
  box?
Bill
Stephen Clark, Holland Park School, Clacton-on-Sea

★ **STAR JOKE** ★ **STAR JOKE** ★ **STAR JOKE** ★

**What do you call a woman who can juggle with pints
  of lager?**
Beatrix

and

What do you call a girl who stands between the goalposts?
Annette
WELL DONE Carolyn Benson, Kingfold School, Penwatham

What do you call a sheep with a machine-gun?
Lambo
Benjamin March, Booker Hill School, High Wycombe

What do you call a woman who sets fire to her bills?
Bernadette
Eleanor Wakeling, Bedgrove School, Aylesbury

What do you call a spy when he goes to bed?
An undercover agent.
Martin Sturdwick, St Joseph's School, Poole

What do you call a flying policeman?
A helicopper.
Samuel Banson, St Mary's School, Hendon

What do you call a man with a seagull on his head?
Cliff
Michelle Gordon, Tilbury Manor School, Tilbury

What do you call a man with a car on his head?
Jack
Cassi Farthing, Weatherby School, Weatherby

What do you call a man with no ears?
Anything you like, he can't hear you.
Daniel Ames, Priory School, Danbury

and finally – what goes . . .

★ STAR JOKE ★ STAR JOKE ★ STAR JOKE ★

What goes peck bang, peck bang, peck bang, peck
   bang?
A chicken in a mine field.
**WELL DONE William Stables, Ranby House School,
   Retford**

15

What goes ninety-nine plonk, ninety-nine plonk, ninety-nine plonk?

A centipede with a wooden leg.

John Skilbeck, Ranby House School, Retford

What goes "Lettuce in"?

A cabbage in a knock knock joke.

Nicola Wealleans, Ryton School, Tyne and Wear

What goes oink clink, oink clink, oink?

A piggy bank.

Katy Roberts, Westfield School, St Ives, Cambridge

Riotous Riddles

There are billions of riddles! Schools are full to bursting with them. The classrooms are overflowing; and the moment the bell rings they all pour out into the playground.

The oldest and worst riddle in the whole world is probably:

Why did the chicken cross the road?
To get to the other side.

No one actually sent that one in (phew!). But there were one or two developments of it. We'll use those to get this first riddle section started:

Why did the one-eyed chicken cross the road?
To get to the Bird's Eye shop.
Nicholas Griffiths, Nicholas Hawksmoor School, Towcester

Why did the cockerel cross the road?
To show that he wasn't chicken.
Matthew Singleton, St Joseph's School, Poole

Why did the hedgehog cross the road?
To see his flatmate.
Guy Rhodes, Ironville & Codnor Park School, Ironville

Why did the dinosaur cross the road?
There weren't any chickens in those days.
Robert Tabor, St Joseph's School, Poole

Why did the man with one hand cross the road?
To get to the second-hand shop.
Nicholas Jackson, Hawes Down School, West Wickham

Why do cows lie down in the rain?
To keep each udder dry.

and

What's yellow and swings from cake to cake?
Tarzipan
Amy Lau, Woodham Ley School, South Benfleet

That reminds me, Amy, of one of my favourites:

What's white and fluffy and swings through the trees?
A meringue-utan.

What do you call a train loaded with toffee?
A chew chew train.
Lee Claft, Mountfield School, Newcastle upon Tyne

Why did the nurse tip-toe past the medicine cupboard?
She didn't want to wake the sleeping pills.
Jaymeena, Horsenden School, Greenford

What dance can you do in the bathroom?
A tap dance.
Clare Gillett, Blackfen School, Sidcup

How many feet in a yard?
It depends how many people are standing in it.
Katherine Burke, Stanway Fiveways School, Colchester

What has a back, two arms, four legs and no body?
An arm chair.
Sarah Toms, St Joseph's School, Poole

What question can never be answered "yes"?
"Are you asleep?"
Michaela Taylor, Ripley Junior, Ripley

What question always receives the answer "yes"?
"How do you pronounce Y.E.S.?"
Nicholas Griffiths, Nicholas Hawksmoor School, Towcester

Why did the boy throw his clock out of the window?
To see if time flies.
Nicholas Jackson, Hawes Down School, West Wickham

What's green and hairy and goes up and down?
A gooseberry in a lift.
Nadia Rahaman, Belleville School, London

What's green and hairy and rides a bike?
A gooseberry that can't afford a car.
Karen Mellan, Linlithgow School, Linlithgow

What bird prepares food?
A cook-coo.
Hayley Newton, Ryton School, Tyne and Wear

★ **STAR JOKE** ★ **STAR JOKE** ★ **STAR JOKE** ★

What do policemen have for lunch?
Truncheon meat sandwiches.
WELL DONE Samantha Christopher, St Joseph's School, Poole

What do hedgehogs have for lunch?
Prickled onions.
Michaela Taylor, Ripley School, Ripley

What is a vampire's favourite food?
Neck-tarines
Stacey Rees, Sheringham School, London

What's pink, has a curly tail and drinks blood?
A hampire.
Amy Wright, St Andrew's School, Dinas Powys

What goes along the bottom of a river at 100 miles an hour?
A motor-pike.
Glen Parrott, Birchwood School, Swanley

What two words have the most letters?
Post Office.
Caroline Green, Bovingdon, Hemel Hempstead

What did the traffic warden have on his bread?
Traffic jam.
Zita Bowler, Farm School, Mansfield

What's yellow on the inside and green on the outside?
A banana dressed up as a cucumber.
Robert Tabor, St Joseph's School, Poole

What's nine feet tall, wrinkled, and likes knitting?
The Incredible Hulk's granny.
Stephanie, St Mary's School, Hendon

Why did the hazlenut go out with a prune?
He couldn't find a date.

and

What do you call two rows of cabbages?
A dual cabbage way.
Joanne Gallagher, Ryton School, Tyne and Wear

What time did the Chinaman visit the dentist?
Tooth hurty.
Sarah Carling, Wetherby School, Wetherby

What is an underground train full of professors called?
A tube of smarties.
Sarah Helliwell, Linlithgow School, Linlithgow

What did the sea say to the beach?
Nothing, it just waved.
Rivinder Purawal, Boleyn Road, Forest Gate

Here are five frog riddles to send you hopping mad:

What happens to a frog's car when it breaks down?
It gets toad away.
Natasha Mendis, St Mary's School, Hendon

What do frogs like to drink?
Croak-a-Cola
Nicholas Jackson, Hawes Down School, West Wickham

What sweets do frogs like?
Lollihops
Derek Bennet, Albany School, Nottingham

Where do frogs put their coats?
In a croak room.
Matthew Boulton, St Peter's School, Broadstairs

Where do frogs keep their money?
In river banks.
Sally Chow, St John's School, Sevenoaks

How do you spell mouse trap using only three letters?
CAT
Sharmila Patel, Elmhurst School, Upton Park

Why did the robber take a bath?
So he could make a clean getaway.
Lynne Reynolds, Westwood School, Welling

What's green and bounces round the garden?
A spring onion
Kelly Jordan, Chilton School, Durham

Where does Tarzan buy his clothes?
A jungle sale.
Joanne Barrow, Albany School, Nottingham

How do ghosts travel abroad?
British Scareways.
Nadia Rahaman, Belleville School, London

What do ghosts eat?
Goulash
Matthew Boulton, St Peter's School, Broadstairs

or

What do ghosts eat?
Spookgetti
Nyree Thornton, St Joseph's School, Poole

What's Chinese and deadly dangerous?
Chop Sueycide.
Joanne Bedford, Wath Central School, Rotherham

How does a witch tell the time?
With a witch-watch.
Cassi Farthing, Wetherby School, Wetherby

★ STAR JOKE ★ STAR JOKE ★ STAR JOKE ★

What do ducks watch on TV?
Duckumentaries.
WELL DONE Krysia Cushing, Ravenstone School, Balham

What's mad and goes to the moon?
A loony module.
Mavelene Ramos, St John Fisher School, Perivale

What gets wetter as it dries?
A towel.
Sarah Toms, St Joseph's School, Poole

How do you make a band stand?
Hide all their chairs.
Annemarie O'Connor, Blackmore School, Essex

★ STAR JOKE ★ STAR JOKE ★ STAR JOKE ★

What's yellow and white and goes down a train track at 100 miles an hour?
A train driver's egg sandwich.

and

What's an Ig?
An Eskimo's house without a toilet.
WELL DONE Joanne Bedford, Wath Central School, Rotherham

What happened to the man who didn't know the difference between putty and toothpaste?
All his windows fell out.
Karen Moss, St John's School, Sidmouth

Why is a baby like an old car?
They both have a rattle.
Vicky Turner, St Joseph's School, Poole

I have ten legs, thirty-six arms and twelve heads, what am I?
A fibber.
Daniel Ames, Priory County School, Danbury

What do you call a penguin in the Sahara desert?
Lost
Karen Mellan, Linlithgow School, Linlithgow

What do you call two robbers?
A pair of nickers.
André Barret, Wetherby School, Wetherby

What goes zzub zzub?
A bee flying backwards.
Nadia Rahaman, Belleville School, London

What four letters scare a robber?
R.I.C.U.
Joanne Bedford, Wath Central School, Rotherham

What happened to the idiot morris dancer?
He fell off the bonnet.
Joanne Barrow, Albany School, Nottingham

What's brave, handsome, and has a very bad memory?
Er . . . I can't remember.
George Moran, Mountfield School, Newcastle upon Tyne

What do you do if the M6 is Closed?
Drive up the M3 twice.
Annemarie O'Connor, Blackmore School, Essex

Where do ghosts go for their holidays?
The Isle of Fright.
Sarah Mercer, Park School, Stonehouse

What's black and white and red all over?
A zebra on a sun bed.
Louise Wilson, Bearpark School, Durham

Mirthful Miscellany

JUDGE: Order! Order in court!
PRISONER: Fish and chips, please, Guv!
Rachael Fryer, Parkroyal School, Macclesfield

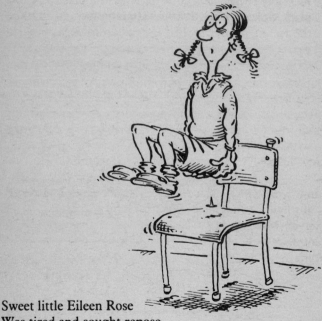

Sweet little Eileen Rose
Was tired and sought repose.
But her naughty sister Clare
Placed a pin upon her chair
And sweet little Eileen rose.
Mary Timothy, St Augustine's School, Nottingham

I went to the pictures tomorrow
I had a front seat at the back
I had a plain cake with currants in
I ate it and gave it her back.
Donna Anderson, St Michael's School, Tettenhall

Thieves have stolen a van full of wigs. The police are combing the area.
Robert Tare, Wetherby School, Wetherby

A lady was sitting next to her friend in a plane. "If this plane turns upside down, would we fall out?" asked the friend. "No," replied the lady. "I'd still speak to you."
Darren Edwards, Carlton School, Boston

I can prove that Moses wore a wig.
How?
Well, sometimes he was seen with Aaron, and sometimes without.
Scott Harvey, Albany School, Nottingham

Jimmy is a very religious boy. He never does homework if there is a Sunday in the week.
Steven Lindsay,
Coatham School,
Redcar

Mary had a little lamb
He had a touch of colic
She gave him brandy twice a day
And now he's alcoholic.
Matthew Bolton, St Joseph's School, Poole

and from the same school:

Mary had a little lamb
It ran around in hops,
It gambolled in the road one day
And ended up as chops.
Christian Richmond, St Joseph's School, Poole

Hey diddle diddle
The cat did a widdle
Right in the middle of the floor.
The little dog laughed to see such fun
And added a little bit more.
Catrina Hunsley, Oatlands School, Harrogate

There was a cowboy in a bar boasting that he was the
    fastest gun in the west. A week later he came in with
    his arm in a sling, and lots of bandages on.
"What happened to you?" asked the people in the bar.
"I got shot," said the cowboy.
"You said you were the fastest gun in the west."
"I am," he replied. "I was on holiday in the east when it
    happened."
Lynne Eastgate, Coton Green School, Tamworth

What did the cow say to her friend?
Moo-ve over.
**Charmone   Smith,   The   Lindens   School,   Sutton
    Coldfield**

32

TEACHER: Tim, can you name a famous explorer?
TIM: Well, Miss, my goldfish – he's been round the globe thousands of times.
Clare Gillet, Blackfen School, Sidcup

Why does a golfer need a spare pair of shoes?
In case he gets a hole in one.
Jamie, St Mary's School, Hendon

DAVID: Sally, you're stupid!
SALLY: Booo hooooo.
DAD: David! That was very unkind; say you're sorry.
DAVID: I'm sorry you're stupid, Sally.
Lisa Tunstall, Ryton School, Tyne and Wear

TEACHER: Give me a sentence with the letter I in it
PUPIL: I is . . .
TEACHER: No, no, it's always "I am."
PUPIL: I am the ninth letter of the alphabet.
Eleanor Wakeling, Bedgrove School, Aylesbury

"I say, waiter, do you serve asparagus?"
"No. We don't serve sparrows and my name's not Gus."
Daniel Ames, Priory School, Danbury

A definition of a net: holes tied together with string!
Samantha Craig, Fir Tree School, Leeds

WALLY: Is this train running on time?
GUARD: No, it's running on rails.
Lynne Reynolds, Westwood School, Welling

My Gran is 80 years old and she hasn't got a grey hair on
her head. She's bald.
Sabih Behzad, St Mary's School, Hendon

GIRL: Where are you going, Mum?
MOTHER: I'm taking your brother to the doctor; I don't like the look of him.
GIRL: I'll come with you – I don't like the look of him either.
Shurwz Ruiz, Mossford Green School, Ilford

JOHN: Look at that bunch of cows.
JANE: Not bunch, herd.
JOHN: Herd what?
JANE: Of cows.
JOHN: Of course I've heard of cows.
Jenny Sherman, Chapel-Le-Ferne School, Folkestone

"Waiter, waiter! I'm in a hurry – will my pancake be long?"
"No, sir, it will be round."
Kerri Williams, Scargill School, Rainham

Ding dong bell
Pussy's in the well,
We put some disinfectant down
And that has cured the smell.
Benjamin Randall, St Joseph's School, Poole

A convict is locked in a cell with only a chair. How does he escape?
He rubs his hands until they are sore, he uses the saw to cut the chair in half. Two halves make a whole. He climbs through the hole and shouts himself hoarse. Then he gets on the horse and gallops away.
Nathan Collquhoun, Mountfield School, Newcastle Upon Tyne

and also

There was a lady stuck down a well. How did she get out?
She had a ladder in her tights.
Janie Johnson, Park School, Stonehouse

TOMMY: I got up last night and shot a tiger in my pyjamas.
MOTHER: What was a tiger doing in your pyjamas?
Siobhan Hart, Oerlinghausen School, Germany

The last words spoken by the fighter pilot: "What does this button do?"
Ian Lan, St Joseph's School, Poole

Once upon a time there were three bears, Daddy bear, Mummy bear and Baby bear. They went for a walk in the woods and when they came back Daddy bear said, "Who's been eating my porridge?" Then Mummy bear said, "Who's been eating my porridge?" Then Baby bear said, "Never mind about the porridge – who's nicked the video."

Kevin Foster, Ushaw Moor School, Durham

★ STAR JOKE ★ STAR JOKE ★ STAR JOKE ★

The Lone Ranger was riding along a desert road when he saw his faithful friend Tonto with his ear close to the ground. The Lone Ranger asked what he was doing.

"Coach with four white horses and carrying five people passed this way!" said Tonto, solemnly.

"How on earth can you tell that, Tonto?" asked the Ranger.

"They just ran over me."

WELL DONE Simon Knevett, Halesworth School, Suffolk

PETER: I just swallowed a fly.
JOHN: Hadn't you better take something for it?
PETER: No, I'll just let it starve to death!

Andrew Etherington, Wetherby School, Wetherby

TEACHER: John, what was the name of the first woman on earth?
JOHN: Give me a clue, Miss.
TEACHER: Think of an apple.
JOHN: Granny Smith, Miss.

Mavelene Ramos, St John Fisher School, Perivale

Three jokes – for the price of one – from Sabih Behzad, St Mary's School, Hendon:

Who was that at the door?
A chap with a drum.
Tell him to beat it.

Who was that at the door?
A man with a wooden leg.
Tell him to hop it.

Who was that at the door?
A lady with a pram.
Tell her to push off.

What's the difference between a television and a newspaper?
Have you ever tried to swot a fly with a television?
Sarah Toms, St Joseph's School, Poole

and another from Sarah:

The Loch Ness monster was swimming around on the bed of Loch Ness, when suddenly he was attacked by six giant squid. He killed them, one by one, and took them under one of his huge flippers to the surface. There he met an old fisherman friend of his. "Here Jock," he said. "Here's the six squid I owe you."

BOY: Grandad, do you move like a frog?
GRANDAD: No, lad, why?
BOY: Well, Dad says we'll get about ten thousand pounds when you hop off.
S. Canige, St Patrick's School, Woolston

Two packets of crisps were walking along the road. A car pulled up and the driver wound down the window. "Would you like a lift?" he asked.

"No thanks," said the crisps, "we're Walkers."

Trevor Stancer, Carlton School, Boston

I saw Esaw sitting on a see-saw. How many Ss in that?

None – in "that".

Clare Constable, Littleport School, Cambridge

MOTHER: Money doesn't grow on trees you know.

DAUGHTER: Well, how come banks have so many branches then?

Natasha Mendis, St Mary's School, Hendon

Knock Knock Jokes

There are trillions of knock knock jokes – and they all got sent in! Here are some of the best.

Knock! Knock!
Who's there?
Ivor
Ivor who?
Ivor you let me in or I'll climb through the window.
Dinuka Athauda, Fairhaven School, Stourbridge

Three great jokes from Derek Bennett, Albany School, Nottingham:

Knock! Knock!
Who's there?
Boo
Boo who?
There's no need to cry, it's only a joke.

and

Knock! Knock!
Who's there?
Sabrina
Sabrina who?
Sabrina long time since I saw you last.

and

Knock! Knock!
Who's there?
Dismay
Dismay who?
Dismay surprise you, but it's only a joke.

Knock! Knock!
Who's there?
Cook
Cook who?
That's the first one I've heard this year.
Katy Roberts, Westfield School, St Ives, Cambridge

42

Knock! Knock!
Who's there?
Tish
Tish who?
Bless you.
Elizabeth Buckingham, Ashford School, Ashford

Knock! Knock!
Who's there?
Snow
Snow who?
Snow good asking me.
Jennifer Adams, Rise Park School, Nottingham

Knock! Knock!
Who's there?
Scott
Scott who?
Scott nothing to do with you.
Derek Bennett, Albany School, Nottingham

Knock! Knock!
Who's there?
Harry
Harry who?
Harry up and open this door.
David Malkin, Oerlinghausen School, Germany

Knock! Knock!
Who's there?
Felix
Felix who?
Felix my lolly once more I'll hit him.
Andrew Etherington, Wetherby School, Wetherby

Knock! Knock!
Who's there?
Dummy
Dummy who?
Dummy a favour and open the door.
Zita Bowler, Farm School, Mansfield

Knock! Knock!
Who's there?
Alec
Alec who?
Alec a nice cup of tea please.
Tara Dixie, St Joseph's School, Poole

Knock! Knock!
Who's there?
Arthur
Arthur who?
Arthur any biscuits?
Stacy Rees, Sheringham School, London

Knock! Knock!
Who's there?
Amos
Amos who?
A mosquito bit me.

and

Knock! Knock!
Who's there?
Andy
Andy who?
Andy bit me again.
Lisa Higgins, Moorlands School, Bath

Knock! Knock!
Who's there?
You
You who?
Did you give me a call?
Dinuka Athauda, Fairhaven School, Stourbridge

★ **STAR JOKE** ★ **STAR JOKE** ★ **STAR JOKE** ★

Knock! Knock!
Who's there?
Adolf
Adolf who?
**Adolf ball hit my dose,
dat's why I talk dis way.**

and

Knock! Knock!
Who's there?
Robin
Robin who?
Robin you, so hand over your money.
WELL DONE Michael Taylor, Ripley School, Ripley

Knock! Knock!
Who's there?
Eggbert
Eggbert who?
Eggbert no bacon thank you.
Sarah Tallent, Albany School, Nottingham

Knock! Knock!
Who's there?
Madam
Madam who?
Madam finger's stuck in the keyhole.
Joanne Gallagher, Ryton School, Tyne and Wear

Knock! Knock!
Who's there?
Police
Police who?
Police let me in, it's cold out here.
Emma Godley, Wetherby School, Wetherby

Knock! Knock!
Who's there?
Guess
Guess who?
It's you that's supposed to be guessing, not me.
Eleanor Wakeling, Bedgrove School, Aylesbury

Knock! Knock!
Who's there?
Wendy
Wendy who?
Wendy red red robin goes bob bob bobbin along.
Carolyn Benson, Kingsfold School, Penwathan

Knock! Knock!
Who's there?
Typhoo
Typhoo who?
No, Typhoo Tea.
Anna Smith, Carlton School, Boston

Knock! Knock!
Who's there?
Les
Les who?
Les go and play cricket.
Mark Ledbury, Oerlinghausen School, Germany

almost finally . . .

Knock! Knock!
Who's there?
Isabel
Isabel who?
Is a bell better than all this knocking.
Michael Scott, Ryton School, Tyne and Wear

absolutely finally . . .

Knock! Knock!
Who's there?
A small boy who can't reach the door bell.
Matthew Toule, Albany School, Nottingham

Monkeys, mice and elephants, and assorted wildlife

Lots of jokes seem to feature animals, so this section is a jungle of jokes. As you would expect there are a large number of elephants, but watch out for the occasional penguin, octopus and even a pink panther!

What's grey and has four legs and a trunk?
A mouse going on holiday.
Jaymeena, Horsenden School, Greenford

There were two mice in an airing cupboard; which one was in the army?
The one near the tank.
James Hammond, Kingsworthy School, Winchester

Did you hear about the man who crossed an elephant with a goldfish?
He got swimming trunks.
Martin Sturdwick, St Joseph's School, Poole

What's grey, has twelve wheels and carries a trunk?
An elephant. I lied about the wheels.
Nicola Hunter, Wetherby School, Wetherby

What's the difference between a letter box and an elephant's bottom?
I don't know.
Well, I hope your mum never sends you out to post a letter.
Cathy Tennent, South Wonston School, Winchester

Why did the elephant wear sunglasses on the beach?
Because he didn't want to be recognized in a crowd!
Jennifer Adams, Rise Park School, Nottingham

How do elephants get down from trees?
They wait until autumn and float down on a leaf!
Ross Wilton, Kingsway, Bath

I thought Ross was going to follow this one with: How
do you get down from an elephant? You don't, you
get down from ducks.

Why are elephants bad dancers?
Because they've got two left feet.
Samantha Craig, Fir Tree School, Leeds

★ STAR JOKE ★ STAR JOKE ★ STAR JOKE ★

A large snake and his son were wiggling their way
across the desert. "Hey, Dad," said the little one,
"are we the really dangerous biting sort of snake –
with deadly venom in our fangs or are we huge bone-
crunching, squeezing, crushing sort of constricting
snakes?"
"We're bone-crunching crushers, son," said his father.
"Thank heavens for that, I just bit my lip."
WELL DONE Richard Taylor, Towyn School, Rhyl

What's the difference between an Indian and an African
elephant?
About 3,000 miles.
Joanne Bedford, Wath Central School, Rotherham

Why aren't elephants allowed on the beach?
Their trunks might fall down.
Chris Shotton, Bearpark School, Durham

SAM: How many elephants can you fit into a matta-booboo?

GEORGE: What's a mattabooboo?

SAM: Nothing, Yogi.

and

What's as big as an elephant, but doesn't weigh anything?

An elephant's shadow.

Mavelene Ramos, St John Fisher School, Perivale

Why don't elephants like penguins?

They can't get the wrappers off.

Richard Meston, St Joseph's School, Poole

What has eight legs, three heads and two tails?

A man sitting on a horse holding a chicken.

Nadia Rahaman, Belleville School, London

How do you stop a fish from smelling?

Cut off its nose.

Amy Midgley, St Peter's School, Darwen

What do you call a shark playing a banjo?
Jaws Formby.
Gareth Glossop, Speedwell School, Staveley

Why did the elephant cross the road?
He wanted to make a trunk call.
Karen Nisbet, Wetherby School, Wetherby

What do mice have that no other animals have?
Baby mice.
Rebecca Dennis, Burwell Village College, Cambridge

When do mice need umbrellas?
When it's raining cats and dogs.
Toni Allsop, Oerlinghausen School, Germany

What would happen if you crossed an elephant with a kangaroo?
Australia would be full of holes.
Scot Wells, St Mary's School, Hendon

What's big and grey and has sixteen wheels?
An elephant on roller skates.
Raymond Stevens, Oerlinghausen School, Germany

A leopard kept on trying to escape from the zoo, but he was always spotted.
Glen Parrott, Birchwood School, Swanley

What do polar bears eat for lunch?
Iceburgers
Krysia Cushing, Ravenstone School, Balham

How does a monkey make toast?
He puts it under a gorilla.
Alexander Vaux, Halstead School, Sevenoaks

What did the Pink Panther say when he trod on an ant?
Dead-ant, dead-ant, dead-ant, dead-ant, dead-ant, dead-ant, dead-ant, dead-ant, dead-ant
Stephen Ranaghan, Wetherby School, Wetherby

Two elephants wanted to go swimming at the same time, but they couldn't because they only had one pair of trunks between them.
Donna Anderson, St Michael's School, Tettenhall

★ STAR JOKE ★ STAR JOKE ★ STAR JOKE ★

A parrot decided to go for a walk, but before leaving the house he put on his raincoat: he wanted to be polyunsaturated.
WELL DONE Rebecca Dennis, Burwell Village College, Cambridge.

How does an octopus go into battle?
Well armed.
Simon, Horsenden School, Greenford

What group of birds is famous for formation flying?
The Red Sparrows.
Stuart Cowell, Oerlinghausen School, Germany

What is parrot food called?
Pollyfilla
Andrew Brookes, St Nicholas School, Radstock

Why is bees' hair always so sticky?
They use honey combs.

and

Where do bees wait for buses?
At buzz stops.
Zita Bowler, Farm School, Mansfield

and finally . . .

How can you tell when there's an elephant in your bed?
Your nose touches the ceiling.
Nicola Roe, Wetherby School, Wetherby

Dogs

Dogs have always been good for a laugh. In fact Susan Ogilvie and Nicola Roane from Oerlinghausen School – a British forces school in Germany – jointly sent in one of the oldest, corniest and best jokes there is:

FIRST MAN: My dog's got no nose.
SECOND MAN: How does he smell?
FIRST MAN: AWFUL

Here are some more

Which type of dog has no tail?
A hot dog.
Bina Mistry, Horseden School, Greenford

How do you stop a dog digging up the garden?
Take his spade away.
Dominic Adamson, Wetherby School, Wetherby

★ **STAR JOKE** ★ **STAR JOKE** ★ **STAR JOKE** ★

**When do spare parts from Japanese cars start falling
out of the sky?**
When it's raining Datsun cogs.
**WELL DONE Amy Lau, Woodham Ley School,
South Benfleet.**

What goes tick woof, tick woof, tick woof, tick woof?
A watch dog.
Kate White, Holland Park School, Clacton-on-Sea

A man went into a pet shop and said to the lady behind
the counter, "Do you have any puppies going cheap?"
"No," said the lady, "they all go woof. Our budgies are
going cheep."
Sharmila Patel, Elmhurst School, Upton Park

What type of dog goes into a corner every time a bell
rings?
A boxer.
Kelly Cox, Cheshire School, RAF Bruggen, Germany

**Three dog jokes from David Parfitt, Earby County
School, Earby**

What kind of dog hides from frying pans?
A sausage dog.

59

What kind of dog goes well with carrots?
A collie dog.

What kind of dog wets the floor?
A poodle.

A man comes out of a fish and chip shop, stands on the pavement and starts eating his fish and chips out of the paper. A lady with a small dog comes across from the other side of the road.

The dog keeps yapping at the man, trying to get at his food.

"Can I throw him a bit?" the man asked the dog owner.

"Certainly," said the lady.

The man picked the dog up and threw it over a wall.

Zoë Robinson, Wetherby School, Wetherby

What do fox hounds like for their lunch?
Fox tail soup.

Corrina Hinchcliffe, Holland Park School, Clacton-on-Sea

What do a dog and a tree have in common?
Bark
Nicola Wealleans, Ryton School, Tyne and Wear

What do you call a dog with a bunch of daisies on its
   head?
A collie-flower.
Lisa Edgley, Wetherby School, Wetherby

and now for some cats

What do you call a cat that works for a doctor?
A first-aid kit.
Kate Neale, Clackclose School, Downham Market

Did you hear about the two ton mouse who walked down a dark alley saying "Here kitty, kitty, kitty."
Ann Coetes, Wetherby School, Wetherby

There were twenty cats in a boat, out at sea. One jumped out. How many cats were left in the boat?
None: they were all copy-cats
Anita Patel, St Mary's School, Hendon

What do you call a disastrous cat?
A catastrophe.
David Reynolds, Fieldcourt School, Quedgeley

What is a cat's favourite TV programme?
Miami Mice.
Ahmer Mohammad, Allerton Grange School, Leeds

Two cat jokes from Caroline Warner, Watling Way School, Milton Keynes that qualify for a

A man took a cat back to a pet shop. "You said this cat would be really good for mice." he complained to the pet shop owner. "I've had it for three weeks and it hasn't caught a single mouse."

"Well," replied the man, "that's good for mice isn't it?"

and

Why do cats change their size?
Because they are let out at night and taken in in the morning.
WELL DONE Caroline.

Ridiculous,
Riotous Riddles

Will the world's supply of riddles ever run out? Will there come a day when everyone will have heard every riddle it's possible to hear? Will there have to be an International Riddle Disaster Fund? I doubt it.

What's the difference betweeen a storm cloud and a child being spanked?
One pours with rain and the other roars with pain.
Steven Burdett, Ryton School, Tyne and Wear

What did the letter say to the stamp?
Stick with me and we'll go places.
Stacy Rees, Sheringham School, London

What Elizabethan explorer could stop bikes?
Sir Francis Brake.
Kenneth Down, Albany School, Nottingham

How do you count cows?
With a cowculator.
Glen Parrott, Birchwood School, Swanley

What would happen if pigs could fly?
Bacon would go up.
Susie Goodwin, Parkroyal School, Macclesfield

A man walked into a bar. What did he say?
Ouch.
Alexis Thompson, St Joseph's School, Poole

What is a horse's favourite sport?
Stable Tennis.
Neil Lucas, Holland Park School, Clacton-on-Sea

How did they know that the Jaws victim had dandruff?
He left his head and shoulders on the beach.
Jocelyn Sissons, Wetherby School, Wetherby

Why are ghosts so bad at lying?
You can see right through them.
Aaron Whelon, St Joseph's School, Poole

What do you call an Irish spider?
Paddy long legs.
Gareth Glossop, Speedwell School, Stavely

What did the traffic lights say to the car?
Don't look, I'm changing.

and

What tools do you use in arithmetic?
Multipliers.
Ravinder Purawal, Boleyn Road, Forest Gate

★ **STAR JOKE** ★ **STAR JOKE** ★ **STAR JOKE** ★

How do you hire a horse?
Stand it on four bricks.
WELL DONE Glen Parrott, Birchwood School, Swanley

How many seconds in a year?
Twelve. January 2nd, February 2nd, etc . . .
Lynne Reynolds, Westwood School, Welling

What car did Tonto drive?
A Lone Range Rover.
Sarah Mercer, Park School, Stonehouse

How do you keep cool at a football match?
Sit next to a fan.
Natasha Mendis, St Mary's School, Hendon

What goes at 100 miles an hour on your washing line?
Hondapants.
Nadia Rahaman, Belleville School, London

Why did the bald man go outside?
To get some fresh hair.
**Nicholas Jackson, Hawes Down School, West
   Wickham**

What do you call a zebra with no stripes?
A horse.
Jamie, St Mary's School, Hendon

What did the tonsil say to the other tonsil?
Put your best clothes on, the doctor's taking us out tonight.
Susan Lee, Holland Park School, Clacton-on-Sea

What gum does J. R. use?
Ewing gum.
Canly Gramlick, Chapel End School, Walthamstow

Who was the first underwater spy?
James Pond.
William Stables, Ranby House School, Retford

What's brown and prickly and squirts jam at you?
A hedgehog eating a doughnut.
Sarah Mercer, Park School, Stonehouse

Where does Kermit keep his money?
In a Miss Piggy bank.
Caroline Green, Bovingdon School, Hemel Hemp-stead

What do you call a robbery in Peking?
A Chinese take-away.
Glen Parrott, Birchwood School, Swanley

What did one eye say to the other?
Between you and me something smells.
Matthew Stafford, Elmstead Market School, Colchester

Why did Batman climb a tree?
To find Robin's nest.
Hayley Newton, Ryton School, Tyne and Wear

What do you give a sick pig?
Oinkment.
Michaela Taylor, Ripley School, Derby

Why did the tomato blush?
Because it saw the salad dressing.
Tom Green, Our Lady's Convent School, Alnwick

When is water not water?
When it's dripping.
Ann Coats, Wetherby School, Wetherby

What's red and stupid?
A blood clot.
Kerri Williams, Scargill School, Rainham

What sort of fish can't swim?
A dead one.
Alexis Thompson, St Joseph's School, Poole

Who wrote Oliver Twist?
How the dickens should I know?.
Daniel Hutchinson, Albany School, Nottingham

Where do snowmen go to dance?
To a snowball.
Kirsty Burton, Oerlinghausen School, Germany

Why do birds fly south in the summer?
It's too far to walk.
Cathy Tennent, South Wonston School, Winchester

Why was the Egyptian girl worried?
Because her daddy was a mummy.
Kay Allen, Mountfield School, Newcastle Upon Tyne

What vegetables are found in boats?
Leeks.
Louise Bohills, Sheringham School, London

What wears shoes but has no feet?
A pavement.
Susan Fleming, River County School, River

What lies under your bed with its tongue hanging out?
Your shoe.
Ross Wilton, Kingsway, Bath

Why is a piano so difficult to open?
All the keys are on the inside.
Michelle Marks, Carlton School, Boston

Why do cows have bells?
Because their horns don't work.
Matthew Stafford, Elstead Market School, Colchester

What is a gardener's favourite game?
Rakes and ladders.
Terry Lumley, Carlton School, Boston

Why are brides unlucky?
Well, they never marry the best man.
Susie Goodwin, Parkroyal School, Macclesfield

How do you make an apple puff?
Chase it round the garden.
Joanne Planinshek, Ryton School, Tyne and Wear

What goes up, but never goes down?
Your age.
Helen, Ravenstone School, Balham

Why did the hedgehog cross the road?
Because it was the chicken's day off.
Wayne Hooper, Hawes Down School, West Wickham

What did the Martian say to the petrol pump?
Take your finger out of your ear when I'm talking to you.
Fleur Bradley, Wetherby School, Wetherby

What's black and white and black and white and black
and white?
A penguin rolling down a hill.
Michelle Marks, Carlton School, Boston

Who speaks at a ghosts' conference?
A spooksman.
Nicholas Griffith, Hawksmoor School, Towcester

How do you get rid of a boomerang?
Throw it down a one-way street.
Tina Williams, Albany School, Nottingham

Why was the cricket team given cigarette lighters?
They had lost all their matches.
Robin Barton, Icknield School, Sawston

Where are the Andies?
On the ends of your armies.
Ashley Williams, Kernsing School, Sevenoaks

What's Dracula's favourite soup.
Scream of tomato.
Amy Wright, St Andrew's School, Dinas Powys

How do you stop a skunk from smelling?
Hold its nose.
Terry Hird, Bearpark School, Durham

Which hand do you stir your tea with?
Neither, I use a spoon.
Simon, Horsenden School, Greenford

What kind of puzzle makes people angry?
A crossword puzzle.
Shamila Patel, Elmhurst School, London

Why did the skeleton run up the tree?
Because a dog was after his bones.
Philip Bibb, Oerlinghausen School, Germany

Why didn't the skeleton go to the disco?
He had no body to go with.
Cassi Farthing, Wetherby School, Wetherby

★ **STAR JOKE** ★ **STAR JOKE** ★ **STAR JOKE** ★

What is green and brown, and if it fell out of a tree
would kill you?
A snooker table.
WELL DONE Julie Fryer, Ryton School, Tyne and
Wear

How does Jack Frost get to work?
By icicle.
Krysia Cushing, Ravenstone School, Balham

What's the fastest bird in Britain?
Sebastian Crow.

and

What do you find in a gum tree?
A stick insect.
Sarah Mercer, Park School, Stonehouse

What nuts can be found in space?
Astronuts.
David Reynolds, Fieldcourt School, Quedgeley

What lies in a pram and wobbles?
A jelly baby.
Glen Parrott, Birchwood School, Swanley

Why does Santa Claus like to work in the garden?
Because he likes to hoe hoe hoe.
Susie Goodwin, Parkroyal School, Macclesfield

More Miscellaneous Mirth

A boastful American from Texas was being shown the sights of London by a taxi driver.

"What's that building there?" asked the Texan.

"That's the Tower of London, sir," replied the taxi driver.

"Say, we can put up a building like that in two weeks back in Texas," drawled the Texan.

A little later he said: "And what's this building we're passing now?"

"It's Buckingham Palace, where the Queen lives."

"Is that so? We could put a building like that up in a week."

A few moments later they were passing Westminster Abbey. "Hey cabbie, what's that building over there?"

"I'm afraid I don't know sir, it wasn't there this morning."

Mark Lunn, Hermitage School, Working

PILOT: May Day! May Day!

CONTROL TOWER: Please state your height and position.

PILOT: I'm about five foot ten, and I'm sitting in the cockpit.

Mavelene Ramos, John Fisher School, Perivale

FATHER: Do you think your teacher likes you?

SON: Oh yes, she likes me a lot.

FATHER: How do you know?

SON: She always puts lots of kisses in my maths book.

Alison Gray, Hawes Down School, West Wickham

BOY: How much am I worth to you, Mum?
HIS MOTHER: You're worth a million pounds to me, son.
BOY: Well, could you lend me five of them?
Rebecca Dennis, Burwell Village College, Cambridge

GIRL: Do you notice any change in me, Mum?
MOTHER: No dear, why should I?
GIRL: I've just swallowed a 5p.
Karen Moss, St John's School, Sidmouth

A boy was sitting at the table with his mum and dad. "I don't like this funny cheese with the holes in," said the boy.

"That's OK, son," said his father, "just eat the cheese and leave the holes."
Kerry Ramsden, Oerlinghausen School, Germany

A man fell 100 feet down a well. His companion was very worried and shouted down to him: "Are you all right? Have you broken anything?"

"No," replied his friend, "there's nothing down here to break."

WELL DONE Teresa Alburey, Albany School, Nottingham

Little Miss Muffet
Sat on a tuffet
Eating her Irish stew
Down came a spider
And sat down beside her
So she went and ate that up too.
Karen Mellan, Linlithgow School, Linlithgow

and another one

78

Little Miss Muffet
Sat on a tuffet
Eating chicken and chips.
Her sister who's hateful
Nicked half a plateful
And strolled away licking her lips.
Vicky Turner, St Joseph's School, Poole

★ STAR JOKE ★ STAR JOKE ★ STAR JOKE ★

A man was walking through a park when he came
across a huge kangaroo. He took it by the paw and
lead it to a policeman.
"What shall I do with this kangaroo, Officer?" he
asked.
"Well, sir, I think you should take it to the zoo."
The next day the policeman saw the man walking with
the kangaroo down the high street.

"I thought I told you to take that kangaroo to the zoo" said the policeman, firmly.

"Well I did," said the man, "And this afternoon I'm taking it to the pictures."

WELL DONE Graham Brown, Wetherby School, Wetherby

A boy who had finished his lunch said "Mum, can I leave the table?"

His mum said, "Yes, dear, I'll save it for your tea."

Stefanie Kinghan, Oerlinghausen School, Germany

CAVEMAN OG: I hear you got hurt in an accident, Ug. What happened?

80

CAVEMAN UG: I sprained my back while hunting dinosaurs.

CAVEMAN OG: What? Did one chase you?

CAVEMAN UG: No, I did it lifting the decoy.

and

My mum says that many years ago she had an extraordinary experience. She had a close encounter with a sub-human, alien creature from outer space, but she never reported it to the authorities. She married it instead.

Robin Barton, Icknield School, Cambridge

My gran fitted roller boots to her rocking chair: she said she wanted to rock and roll.

Louise Dunbavin, St Laurence School, Birmingham

A plumber went into a garden: to mend the leeks.

Jane Holland, Riddings School, Derby

two teddy bear jokes from Wetherby School

What is a teddy bear's favourite drink?
Ginger bear.
Jessica Thompson

What's the best way to catch a teddy bear?
Ask someone to throw it to you.
Nicola Roe

Three men were marooned on a desert island, and they
were each granted a wish. The first two men wished
to be back at home with their families. The third man
thought about his wish. "I am lonely," he said, "I
wish my two friends were here with me."
Kerri Williams, Scargill School, Rainham

One day little Kevin was helping his brother clean his
car.
"What's this L mean?" he asked.
"It means I'm a learner."
"Oh, and does this GB mean Getting Better?"
Lisa Tunstall, Ryton School, Tyne and Wear

I have six legs, two bodies, fifteen eyes, three noses and
fifty fingers on each hand. What am I?
Ugly.
Alexis Thompson, St Joseph's School, Poole

DOCTOR: Please face the window and put your tongue
out.
PATIENT: Will that help to cure me?
DOCTOR: No, but I don't like the man who lives opposite.
**George Moran, Mountfield School, Newcastle upon
Tyne**

Words on the headstone of a robot's grave: Rust In Peace.
Jennifer Adams, Rise Park School, Nottingham

Who invented the first plane that could not fly?
The Wrong brothers.
Rachael Fryer, Parkroyal School, Macclesfield

A boy was cutting a cake. He cut it into one small piece, and one huge piece; then he took the huge piece and put it on his plate.

"That's very bad mannered!" said the girl. "If I had cut the cake I would have taken the smaller piece."

"Well, that's all right, you've got it anyway!" said the horrible boy.
Joanne Planinshek, Ryton School, Tyne and Wear

A farmer in Kent has a lovely plum tree. The main trunk has twenty-four branches, each branch has twelve boughs and each bough has six twigs. There's one fruit on each twig. How many apples are there on the tree?

None – it's a plum tree.

Michaela Taylor, Ripley School, Derby

A boy was seen by his father burying his radio in the garden. "What are you doing son?" he asked.

"I'm burying my radio – the batteries are dead."

Glen Parrott, Birchwood School, Swanley

Two flies were playing football in a saucer; they were practising for the cup.

Gareth Glossop, Speedwell School, Staveley

There were three pieces of string, and they all wanted a drink. The first went into a pub and asked for some beer but the barmaid said, "Sorry, we only serve humans." The next piece of string went into the pub and the same thing happened. The third piece of string quickly tied himself into a knot and unravelled his ends. The barmaid said, "We don't serve punks, are you a punk?"

"No," said the piece of string, "I'm a frayed knot."
Katherine Burke, Stanway Fiveways School, Colchester

★ **STAR JOKE** ★ **STAR JOKE** ★ **STAR JOKE** ★

TAXI DRIVER: **Please could you just look and tell me if my indicator winkers are working?**
PASSENGER: **Yes . . . no . . . yes . . . no . . . yes . . . no . . . yes . . . no . . .**
WELL DONE Mavelene Ramos, St John Fisher School, Perivale

Two prunes were arrested yesterday for being stewed.
They were remanded in custardy.
Krysia Cushing, Ravenstone School, Balham

I can make you talk like a Red Indian.
How?
See, I told you.
Sarah Tallent, Albany School, Nottingham

PATSY: I bet I can make you say the word black.
MIKE: Go on then.
PATSY: What are the colours in the Union Jack?
MIKE: Red, white and blue.
PATSY: There you are – I said I'd make you say blue.
MIKE: No – you said black.
PATSY: You've said it.
Clare Constable, Littleport School, Littleport, Cambridge

★ STAR JOKE ★ STAR JOKE ★ STAR JOKE ★

FATHER: Well, son, how are your exam marks?
SON: They're under water
FATHER: What do you mean?
SON: Below C level.

and

FIRST MUM: What's your lad going to be when he's passed his exams?
SECOND MUM: The way he's going, a pensioner I should think.

WELL DONE Steven Lindsay, Coatham School, Redcar

TEACHER: Sammy, if you were in a boat and a storm came up, what would you do?

SAMMY: Put an anchor out.

TEACHER: What would you do if another storm came up?

SAMMY: Put out another anchor.

TEACHER: Hey. Where are you getting all these anchors from?

SAMMY: Where are you getting all these storms from?

Asim, St Mary's School, Hendon

A little girl's Nan said to her, "Eat up your greens, or you won't grow up to be a beautiful lady." The little girl looked up at her and said, "Didn't you eat your greens then?"

Neil Lennan, St Joseph's School, Poole

Have You Heard?

How many times have you heard someone in the playground about to begin a joke with "Have you heard the one about . . ."?

Here are some you may or may not have heard!

Have you heard the one about butter?
Don't spread it.
Elizabeth Webb, Blackfen School, Sidcup

Have you heard the joke about the very high wall?
I won't tell you – you'd never get over it.
Andrew Notman, Albany School, Nottingham

Have you heard about the Irish woodworm?
He was found dead in a brick.
Benjamin Clarke, National School, Hucknall

Did you hear about the man who bought a paper shop?
It blew away.
Darren Ungless, Albany School, Nottingham

Did you hear about the fight in the box of biscuits?
A bandit hit a penguin with a club, tied him up with a blue ribbon and got away in a taxi.
Annemarie O'Connor, Blackmore School, Essex

Did you hear about the man who asked his son what was on the telly?

The boy replied, "Only the goldfish bowl and the photo of mum, as usual."
Stacey Rees, Sheringham School, London

Have you heard about crocodiles' favourite card game?
Snap.
Daniel Ames, Priory School, Danbury

Have you heard about the cross-eyed teacher?
He couldn't control his pupils.
Susan Fleming, River County School, River

Have you heard about the farmer who ploughed his field with a steam roller?
He wanted to grow mashed potatoes.
Jennifer Adams, Rise Park School, Nottingham

Did you hear about the orange that got stuck on the road?
It had run out of juice.
Louise Hickey, Holland Park School, Clacton-on-Sea

Did you hear about the man who went to the doctor and told him that he felt as if he was a suitcase?
The doctor soon sent him packing.
Katy Morfett, Archbishop of York's School, York

Have you heard about the sick gnome?
He went to the Elf Centre.
Anna Midgley, St Peters School, Darwen

Have you heard about my Gran?
Her teeth are like stars – they come out at night.
Matthew Stafford, Elmstead Market School, Colchester

Have you heard about the eskimo who found a way to keep the roof on his house?
Iglood it.
Tina Williams, Albany School, Nottingham

Have you heard about the boy who took a pencil to bed?
He said it was so he could draw the curtains.
Reshma, St Mary's School, Hendon

Incidentally, have you heard the story about the broken
  pencil?
I'd better not tell it to you – there's no point to it.
Joanne Planinshek, Ryton School, Tyne and Wear

Have you heard what the policeman said to his belly-
  button?
"You're under a vest."
Sarah Tallent, Albany School, Nottingham

Have you heard about the really cruel school cook?
She used to beat the eggs and whip the cream.
Gillian Blyth, Oerlinghausen School, Germany

Did you hear about the cowboy who never had any money?

His name was Skint Eastwood.

Anouska Laming, Park School, Stonehouse

Have you heard about the man who was sitting on a park bench with a carrot in each ear?

A woman came up to him and said, "Excuse me, but you've got a carrot sticking in each ear."

He said, "I'm sorry, I can't hear you – I've got a carrot sticking in each ear."

Jane Holland, Riddings School, Derby

Have you heard about the boy who, for homework, had to name six things that contained milk?

He put chocolate, rice pudding, ice cream and three cows.

Steven Lindsay, Coatham School, Redcar

Did you hear about the policeman who stopped a tortoise on the M1?

He said to it, "What do you think you are doing on the motorway?"

The tortoise said, "About 1 metre per hour."

Mary Shore, Holland Park School, Clacton-on-Sea

Have you heard about the police patrol car driver who called on his mother?

He knocked on the door and she called out, "Who is it?"

He replied, "It's meema meema meema meema."

Natalie Willey, Albany School, Nottingham

Did you hear what the big telephone said to the little one?

"You're too young to be engaged."

Annie, St Mary's School, Hendon

Have you heard about the code message that is the same from left to right, right to left, upside down and the right way up?

S.O.S.

Sharmila Patel, Elmhurst School, London

Have you heard about my Auntie Muriel?

She received a letter one day and when she read it she burst into tears. "What's the matter?" we asked her.

"Oh dear," she sobbed. "It's my favourite nephew – he's growing up deformed. He's got three feet."

"Three feet."

"Yes, his mother has just written to say that he's grown another foot."

Cheryl Swain, Albany School, Nottingham

Have you heard about the girl who asked her mum if she could have an apple?

"Another apple?" her mother replied. "Apples don't grow on trees, you know."

Leanne Talbot, Oerlinghausen School, Germany

Did you hear about the silly man who cut a hole in the fence of a nudist camp?

The police are looking into it.

Martin Sturdwick, St Joseph's School, Poole

★ STAR JOKE ★ STAR JOKE ★ STAR JOKE ★

Did you hear what happened to the girl who slept with her head under her pillow?

The fairies came and took out all her teeth.

WELL DONE Elaine Cheung, Stanway Fiveways School, Colchester

Have you heard about Big Chief Running Water?

He had two sons, so he called them Hot and Cold.

Joanne Bedford, Wath Central School, Rotherham

Have you heard the one about the boys fighting in the playground?

The teacher separated them and told them that they shouldn't behave like that: "You must learn to give and take," she said.

"We do, Miss," said one of them. "I gave him a thump and he took my apple."

Rebecca Dennis, Burwell Village College, Cambridge

Two terrible jokes from Carolyn Benson, Kingsfold School, Penwatham

Did you hear about the fellow with wooden legs?
He caught fire and burnt to the ground.

Have you heard about the man who was lying in a hospital bed?

"Oh, Doctor," he said, "I can't feel my legs."

"I'm not surprised," said the doctor, "I've cut your arms off."

Have you heard about the man who wanted to dance and cut his toe-nails at the same time?

He invented the sword dance.

Natasha Mendis, St Mary's School, Hendon

Did you hear about the ugly man who sent his photograph to the Lonely Hearts Club?

They sent it back and said they weren't that lonely.

Lynne Reynolds, Westwood School, Welling

Did you hear about the boy who turned up at school with only one glove on?

The teacher asked him why. He said, "Well, the weather forecast said that it might be warm, but on the other hand it might be quite cool."

Steven Lindsay, Coatham School, Redcar

Did you hear the one about the cornflakes?

I'll tell you next week – it's a cereal.

Elizabeth Webb, Blackfen School, Sidcup

and finally

Do you know the one about the dustbin?

I won't tell you, it's absolute rubbish.

Joanne Gallagher, Ryton School, Tyne and Wear

Even More Ridiculous, Riotous Riddles

I was going to start this section by asking you the one about shark infested custard, but as Michelle Heming of Albany School, Nottingham points out – you'd never swallow it.

So here's a good one to begin with

★ STAR JOKE ★ STAR JOKE ★ STAR JOKE ★

How do you keep a twit in suspense?
I'll tell you later.
WELL DONE Susan Fleming, River County School, River

Why is a banana skin on a pavement like music?
Because if you don't C sharp you'll B flat.
Lorna Pring, Derby School, Osnabrück, Germany

What skeleton was Emperor of France?
Napoleon Bone-apart.
Amy Wright, St Andrew's School, Dinas Powys

What group of heroes protect farmers?
The Hay Team.
Kenneth Down, Albany School, Nottingham

Who invented fire?
Some bright spark.
Jennifer Adams, Rise Park School, Nottingham

Why did they build the Forth Bridge?
Because the third one fell down.
Alexis Thompson, St Joseph's School, Poole

What were Tarzan's last words?
"Who greased this vine?"
Andrew Etherington, Wetherby School, Wetherby

Why can't cars play football?
They only have one boot.
Sheela Patade, Horsenden School, Greenford

Which burns longer, a black candle or a white candle?
Neither: they both burn shorter.
Katherine Burke, Stanway Fiveways School, Colchester

What can you put in a barrel to make it lighter?
A hole.
Simon, Horsenden School, Greenford

What kind of ears do engines have?
Engineers.
Rebecca Dennis, Burwell Village College, Cambridge

What kind of crisps fly?
Plane crisps.
Elizabeth Buckingham, Ashford School, Ashford

Who can shave seven times a day and still have a beard?
A barber.
Susan Goodwin, Parkroyal School, Macclesfield

Why do bees hum?
Because they don't know the words.
Matthew Stafford, Elmstead Market School, Colchester

What has twelve legs, six ears, but only one eye?
Three blind mice and half a kipper.
Ross Wilton, Kingsway, Bath

What wobbles when it flies?
A jellycopter.
David Rogers, Evenlode School, Penarth

What kind of clothes did people wear during the Great Fire of London?
Blazers.
Louise Bohills, Sheringham School, London

What's the difference between a jeweller and a jailer?
One sells watches and the other watches cells.
John, Mountfield School, Newcastle upon Tyne

Why did the orange stop in the middle of the road?
It wanted to play squash with the cars.
Anitie Sharma, Downshall School, Ilford

What did the priest say when he saw insects on his flowers?
Let us spray.
Jane Ladd, St Joseph's School, Ross-on-Wye

What would you do with a sick wasp?
Take it to a waspital.
Cathy Tennent, South Wonston School, Winchester

Why is a policeman strong?
Because he can hold up the traffic with one hand.
Glyn Hughes, St Joseph's School, Poole

What does an executioner write?
A chopping list.
Andrew Etherington, Wetherby School, Wetherby

What sort of lights did Noah's Ark have?
Floodlights.
Daniel Hutchinson, Albany School, Nottingham

What happened to the man who stole a calendar?
He got twelve months.
Steven Hodgson, Bearpark School, Durham

Where would a sleepy man post a letter?
In a pillow-box.
Louise Rollinson, Albany School, Nottingham

What's got a bottom at the top of it?
A leg.
Lisa Higgins, Moorlands School, Bath

What's green and holds up stage coaches?
Dick Gerkin.
David Bowers, Witney School, Witney

What do you get if you cross Miss Piggy with itching
  powder?
Pork scratchings.
Victoria Ladds, Carlton School, Boston

What can you eat in Paris?
The Trifle Tower.
Danny Crowther, Blackfen School, Sidcup

Why does a flamingo lift up one leg?
If it lifted them both it would fall in the water.
Simon, Horsenden School, Greenford

★ **STAR JOKE** ★ **STAR JOKE** ★ **STAR JOKE** ★

What does a vampire have for breakfast?
Readyneck.

and . . .

What does a cat have for breakfast?
Mice Crispies.

**WELL DONE Ahmer Mohammad, Allerton Grange
  School, Leeds**

Where do policemen live?
999 Letsby Avenue.
Gary Cooper, Bearpark School, Durham

What's big and hairy and flies to America?
King Kongcord.
Amy Wright, St Andrew's School, Dinas Powys

What's the nearest thing to silver?
The Lone Ranger's bottom.
Michelle Newton, Carlton School, Boston

How do you make Barry Manilow's nose five miles long?
Fold it in half.
Claire Perry, Moorlands School, Bath

What did stone-age men like listening to?
Rock music.
Glen Parrott, Birchwood School, Swanley

Where was Sir Lancelot trained?
At night school.
Kelvin Janson, Albany School, Nottingham

What do you say to a three-headed policeman?
Hello, hello, hello.
Mathew Stafford, Elmstead Market School, Colchester

What do you call a cow that eats your grass?
A lawn mooer.
Lindsay Curry, Bearpark School, Durham

What's the difference between a bargain hunter and a sailor?
One goes to see the sales, and one goes to sail the seas.
Sheela Patade, Horsenden School, Greenford

What's old, pink and wrinkly and belongs to Grandad?
Grandma.
Jonathan Carr, Hartside School, Crook

What lives at the bottom of the sea and shakes?
A nervous wreck.
Robin Barton, Icknield School, Sawston

Why can't you hang a man with a wooden leg?
You'd never get it round his neck.
Scott Harvey, Albany School, Nottingham

What did the baby chicken say when its mother laid an orange?
Look what mama laid.

and

Who are fish scared of?
Jack the Kipper.
Stephen Cherrett, St Joseph's School, Poole

What sleeps at the bottom of the sea?
A kipper.
Glen Parrott, Birchwood School, Swanley

What kind of umbrella does the Queen use when it's
raining?
A wet one.
Kelly Cox, RAF School Bruggen, Germany

How do you make a sausage roll?
Push it.
Joanne Bedford, Wath Central School, Rotherham

What does minimum mean?
A very small mum.
Maria Boyle, Wetherby School, Wetherby

Spell hungry horse in four letters.
M.T.G.G.
Claire Perry, Moorlands School, Bath

If a crocodile ˜kin makes a pair of shoes, what do you
make from banana skins?
Slippers.

and

What do you get in newspapers on Fridays?
Fish and chips.
Anouska Laming, Park School, Stonehouse

What's purple and hums?
An electric plum.
Karen Moss, St John's School, Sidmouth

What did the curtain say to the other curtain?
Well, I'll be hanged.
Dion Sherwood, Pyrcroft School, Chertsey

What happened when Moses had a headache?
God gave him some tablets.
Sharon James, St Joseph's School, Poole

What paper do secret agents use?
Basildon Bond.
Matthew Singleton, St Joseph's School, Poole

How do you start a teddy bear race?
Ready! Teddy! Go!
Sarah Tallent, Albany School, Nottingham

Where does the General keep his armies?
Up his sleevies.
Susie Goodwin, Parkroyal School, Macclesfield

Doctor, Doctor

There are zillions of doctor jokes – and here are some of the very best. They are particularly good to read when you are ill, or in hospital. If you've just had an operation they'll have you in stitches.

One of my favourites is

Doctor, Doctor, I think I'm shrinking.
Well, you'll just have to be a little patient.

Now for some of yours

Doctor, Doctor, I keep thinking I'm a telephone.
Well, take these pills and if you don't get better give me a ring.
Lindsay Curry, Bearpark School, Durham

Doctor, Doctor, I think I need glasses.
You certainly do; this is a fish and chip shop.
WELL DONE Nicholas Griffith, Nicholas Hawksmoor School, Towcester

Doctor, Doctor, I feel very crummy.
I think you must be off your loaf.
Katy Morfett, Archbishop of York's School, York

Doctor, Doctor, I keep thinking I'm a goat.
How long have you felt like this?
Since I was a kid.
Steven Hodgeson, Bearpark School, Durham

Doctor, Doctor, I've swallowed a spoon.
Well, sit over there and don't stir.
Jennifer Leech, Holland Park School, Clacton-on-Sea

Doctor, Doctor, I think I've got double vision, how can I cure it?

Go around with one eye shut.

Robin Barton, Icknield School, Sawston

Doctor, Doctor, I just can't get to sleep at night.

Don't worry; move nearer the edge of your bed – you'll soon drop off.

David Shotton, Bearpark School, Durham

Doctor, Doctor, everyone keeps putting me in the dustbin.

Don't talk rubbish.

Simon Townsend, Park School, Stonehouse

★ STAR JOKE ★ STAR JOKE ★ STAR JOKE ★

Doctor, Doctor, my wooden leg is giving me a lot of pain.

Why's that?

My wife keeps hitting me over the head with it.

WELL DONE Kiran Dattani, Horsenden School, Greenford

Doctor, Doctor, I keep thinking I'm the invisible man.

Well, I can't see you now.

Fleur Bradley, Wetherby School, Wetherby

Doctor, Doctor, I've only got 59 seconds to live.

Wait a minute, please.

Wayne Hooper, Hawes Down School, West Wickham

Doctor, Doctor, people keep ignoring me.

Next

Gary Cooper, Bearpark School, Durham

Doctor, Doctor, I think I'm a fly.
Well, buzz off then.
Helen, Ravenstone School, Balham

Doctor, Doctor, I think I'm a pack of cards.
Sit down, I'll deal with you later.
Claire Ballinger, Oerlinghausen School, Germany

Doctor, Doctor, everything I swallow comes up.
Quick – swallow my soccer coupon.
Mavelene Ramos, St John Fisher School, Perivale

Doctor, Doctor, I have this terrible dream where I'm
trying to get through a door with a sign on it, and I
push and push and I can't get through.
Really? How strange. What does the sign say?
Pull.
Rachel Unthank, Ryton School, Tyne and Wear

Doctor, Doctor, I think I'm a banana.
Well, slip over there and peel your clothes off.
Tom Green, Our Lady's Convent School, Alnwick

Doctor, Doctor, I think I'm a pair of curtains.
Well, pull yourself together then.
Elizabeth Webb, Blackfen School, Sidcup

DOCTOR: Did you take your medicine followed by a nice
  hot bath, like I told you?
PATIENT: Well, Doctor, I swallowed the medicine OK,
  but I didn't manage to finish all the bath.
Terry Hird, Bearpark School, Durham

Doctor, Doctor, my family think I'm mad.
Why?
Because I like sausages.
There's nothing mad about that, I like sausages too.
Do you? You should come over to my place then and see
  my collection – I've got thousands.
Lisa Howes, Tolcarne School, Penzance

Doctor, Doctor, I'm really scared about this operation you are going to give me.
Oh don't worry – in all my experience doing surgery only one patient has ever died.
How many people have you operated on?
You're my second.
David Reynolds, Fieldcourt School, Quedgeley

Doctor, Doctor, I think I'm an apple.
Well, sit down over here – I won't bite you.
Julie Fryer, Ryton School, Tyne and Wear

and two more from Gary Cooper at Bearpark School, Durham

Doctor, Doctor, I keep thinking I'm a bridge.
Now then, what's come over you?
Three cars and a bus.

and

Doctor, Doctor, I think I'm a snooker ball.
Well, wait at the end of the cue.

Doctor, Doctor, my head has flowers and trees growing out of it, and people keep having picnics on me.
Ahh. I expect you've got a beauty spot.
Elizabeth Webb, Blackfen School, Sidcup

Doctor, Doctor, I keep feeling that I'm a dog.
Well, sit down and tell me about it.
I can't. I'm not allowed on the furniture.
Karen Goodwin, Wetherby School, Wetherby

Doctor, Doctor, my hair keeps falling out. Can you give me something to keep it in?
Yes, a paperbag.
Krysia Cushing, Ravenstone School, Balham

Even More

This section of mixed jokes rounds off our collection. Thanks again to all those people who sent in so many great jokes.

TEACHER: Now then, you are new here. What is your name?

NEW BOY: Albert Micky Jones.

TEACHER: I see. Well, I'll call you Albert Jones then.

NEW BOY: My dad won't like that.

TEACHER: Why not?

NEW BOY: He doesn't like people taking the Micky out of my name.

Deniz Ibrahim, Dog Kennel Hill School, London

Here is a newsflash: the man who was knocked down in the highstreet by a steam roller today is now in hospital. He can be visited in wards eight, nine and ten.
Michael Norrish, Albany School, Nottingham

Poor old teacher. We missed you so
When into hospital you had to go.
For you to remain there will be a sin:
We're sorry about the banana skin.
Robin Barton, Icknield School, Sawston

I'd like to have your picture,
It would look very nice.
I'd put it in the cellar,
To frighten all the mice.
Benjamin Randall, St Joseph's School, Poole

Quasimodo was ringing the bells in a church when a man came in and offered to help him. The first time the man pulled a rope he shot up in the air and was thrown straight out of the window.

Quasimodo rushed downstairs to the street where a policeman was bending over the injured man. "Do you know this man, sir?" the policeman asked Quasimodo. "No," replied the hunchback, "he doesn't ring a bell."
Tamara Lambourne, Witney School, Witney

If a circular wood is two miles across, how far can you go into it?
Only a mile – after that you are coming out.
Michaela Taylor, Ripley School, Ripley

PUPIL: I've finished the exam, sir.

TEACHER: Good. Did the questions give you any trouble?
PUPIL: No, but some of the answers did.
Susan Fleming, River County School, River

A lorry driver was going down a one-way street the wrong way and a policeman saw him. Why didn't he arrest him?
Because the lorry driver was walking.
Che Binder, Albany School, Nottingham

Keep Britain tidy. Post your rubbish abroad.
Benjamin Randall, St Joseph's School, Poole

Newsflash: Police have just reported the theft of a lorry full of prunes. They are looking for a man on the run.
Carrie Goodall, Albany School, Nottingham

"I'll pay you 20p to clean my car this week," said Mr Jones to John, "and if you do it next week I'll raise it to 30p."

"Great," said John, "I'll start next week."

Rebecca Dennis, Burwell Village College, Cambridge

JIM: I'm sorry I'm late for school; I was having a dream about football.

TEACHER: Why does having a dream about football make you late for school?

JIM: They played extra time.

Steven Lindsay, Coatham School, Redcar

Teachers are special because they are in a class of their own.

Anouska Laming, Park School, Stonehouse

She stood on the bridge at midnight,
Her lips were all a-quiver,
She gave a cough
Her leg dropped off,
And floated down the river.

Mark Lunn, Hermitage County School, Woking

MATTHEW: Can you come out to play, John?

JOHN: No, sorry, I'm helping my dad do my homework.

Matthew Boulton, St Peter's School, Broadstairs

And another one rather like it

FATHER: Do you want some help with your homework Son?

BOY: No thanks, Dad, I'll get it wrong on my own.

Steven Lindsay, Coatham School, Redcar

GIRL: Last night I opened the door in my nightie.
HER FRIEND: That's a funny place to have a door.
Elaine Cheung, Stanway Fiveways School, Colchester

DINER: Waiter. What is wrong with my eggs?
WAITER: I don't know, sir. I only lay the tables.
Sheela Patade, Horsenden School, Greenford

Old Mother Hubbard went to the cupboard to give her
    poor doggy a bone. When she got there she said,
    "O.I.C.U.R.M.T."
Michaela Taylor, Ripley School, Ripley

Hickory Dickory Dock
The elephant ran up the clock.
The clock is now being repaired.
Robin Barton, Icknield School, Sawston

One day little Sandra was playing in the park with her
   big sister. She insisted that she wanted to run along
   the top of a big wall. "If you fall off," said her sister,
   "and break both your legs, don't come running to me
   for sympathy."
Lisa Tunstall, Ryton School, Tyne and Wear

NOW SOME FAVOURITE LIMERICKS

I sat next to a Duchess at tea,
It was just as I feared it would be.
Her rumbling abdominal
Was simply phenomenal,
And everyone thought it was me.
Susie Goodwin, Parkroyal School, Macclesfield

A charming young singer called Hanna
Got caught in a flood in Savanna.
She floated away,
Her sister – they say,
Accompanied her on the pianna.
Mark Lunn, Hermitage County School, Woking

★ **STAR JOKE** ★ **STAR JOKE** ★ **STAR JOKE** ★

There was a young lady from Surrey,
Who cooked up a large pot of curry.
She ate the whole lot,
Straight from the pot,
And ran to the tap in a hurry.
WELL DONE Raymond Stevens, Oerlinghausen
** School, Germany**

There was an old lady from Spain,
Who couldn't go out in the rain,
'Cos she lent her umbrella
To Queen Isabella,
Who never returned it again.
David Bowers, Witney School, Witney

There was a young man from Bengal,
Who went to a fancy dress ball,
He thought he would risk it

123

And go as a biscuit,
But a dog ate him up in the hall.
Sabih Behzad, St Mary's School, Hendon

There was an old lady from Niger
Who went for a ride on a tiger,
No sooner than that,
The tiger got fat,
With the lady from Niger inside her.
Lynne Eastgate, Coton Green School, Tamworth

To finish this section an excellent "Teddy Bear Manual" sent in by Sarah Mercer, Park School, Stonehouse, which qualifies for a

★ STAR JOKE ★ STAR JOKE ★ STAR JOKE ★

TEDDY BEAR OPERATING MANUAL

1 If Teddy feels hard and smooth and stiff you have not yet taken him out of his box. Remove at once.

2 Check to make sure that his ears are in position at the top of bear. If his bottom is on top you are holding him upside-down.

3 To get upside-down bear the right side up take him in right hand and rotate until his ears come to the top (or you could try standing on your head).

4 Do not plug Teddy into nearest electric socket. What are you, some kind of lunatic?

5 Give Teddy a test hug. If on first squeeze bear still feels hard and smooth you are hugging the box. Can't you get rid of that silly box?

6 If on the next hug Teddy squeals and licks your ear, you have picked up the dog.

7 Don't forget to clean Teddy after every hundred thousand hugs.

WELL DONE Sarah

THE COMPILER WOULD LIKE TO THANK
BOOKS FOR STUDENTS, BIRD ROAD,
WARWICK, FOR COLLECTING ALL THE
JOKES USED IN THIS BOOK, AND THE
TEACHERS RUNNING SCHOOL PAPERBACK
SHOPS WHO HELPED THEM.